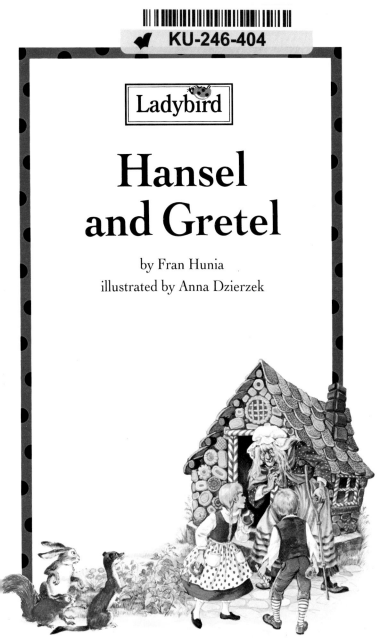

KU-246-404

Ladybird

Hansel and Gretel

by Fran Hunia
illustrated by Anna Dzierzek

Here are
Hansel and Gretel.

Hansel and Gretel's father is a woodcutter.

The stepmother says, We have no food. Hansel and Gretel have to go.

No, says the woodcutter.

The stepmother says, Yes. They have to go.

The woodcutter
and the stepmother
go to sleep.

Hansel gets up.

He looks
for some pebbles.

In the morning
they go out
to get some wood.

Hansel drops
the pebbles
as they go.

The woodcutter
lights a fire.

You stay here,
Hansel and Gretel,
he says.
We are going to look
for some wood.

Hansel and Gretel
go to sleep.

The woodcutter
and the stepmother
go home.

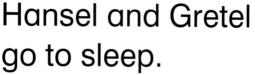

The fire
has gone out.

Hansel and Gretel
get up.

They look
for the pebbles.

Look, says Hansel.
Here are the
pebbles.
We can go home.

Hansel and Gretel
go home.

The woodcutter
jumps up.
Hansel and Gretel!
he says.
It is good to
have you home.

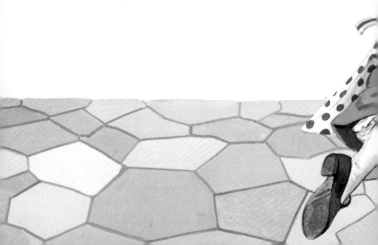

The woodcutter says
to the stepmother,
I want Hansel
and Gretel
to stay here.

No, says
the stepmother.
We have no food.
Hansel and Gretel
have to go.

The woodcutter and
the stepmother
go to sleep.

Hansel gets up
to look
for some pebbles.

He can't get out.

In the morning
they go out
to get some wood.

Hansel has
no pebbles.

He drops
some breadcrumbs.

The woodcutter
lights a fire.
Stay here,
Hansel and Gretel,
he says.
We are going to
get some wood.

Hansel and Gretel
go to sleep.
The woodcutter
and the stepmother
go home.

The fire is out.
Hansel and Gretel
get up.

They want to go home.

They look
for the breadcrumbs.

The breadcrumbs
have gone.

Hansel and Gretel
can't go home.

Hansel and Gretel
come to a house.

Gretel says,
This house is good
to eat.

They eat and eat.

A witch comes out.
You can come in,
says the witch.

The witch wants to eat
Hansel and Gretel.

The witch puts Hansel
into a cage.

The witch lights
a fire.

Is the fire hot?
says the witch
to Gretel.

It looks hot,
says Gretel.
Come and have a look.

The witch looks
into the fire.

In you go,
says Gretel.

Gretel says, Hansel!
The witch is in the fire!
We can go home.

Look, says Hansel.
Here is
some treasure.
We can have it.

They get the treasure,
and find the way home.

The stepmother
has gone.

The woodcutter says,
Hansel and Gretel,
it is good
to have you home.

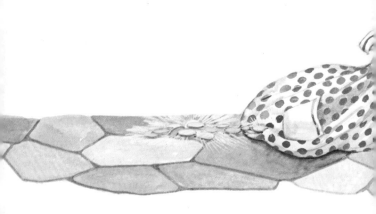

LADYBIRD
READING SCHEMES

Read It Yourself links with all Ladybird reading
schemes and can be used with any other method
of learning to read.

Say the Sounds

Ladybird's **Say the Sounds** graded reading scheme is a
phonics scheme. It teaches children the sounds of individual
letters and letter combinations, enabling them to tackle new
words by building them up as a blend of smaller units.

There are 8 titles in this scheme:

1 **Rocket to the jungle**
2 **Frog and the lollipops**
3 **The go-cart race**
4 **Pirate's treasure**
5 **Humpty Dumpty and the robots**
6 **Flying saucer**
7 **Dinosaur rescue**
8 **The accident**

Support material available: Practice Books, Double Cassette pack,
Flash Cards